Stone the Crows,
it's a Vacuum-cleaner

Bob Wilson

Best Friends · Jessy Runs Away · **Rachel Anderson**
Changing Charlie · **Scoular Anderson**
Weedy Me · **Sally Christie**
Something Old · **Ruth Craft**
Almost Goodbye Guzzler · Two Hoots · **Helen Cresswell**
Magic Mash · Nina's Machines · **Peter Firmin**
Shadows on the Barn · **Sarah Garland**
Clever Trevor · **Brough Girling**
Private Eye of New York · **Nigel Gray**
The Thing-in-a-Box · **Diana Hendry**
Desperate for a Dog · Houdini Dog · **Rose Impey**
Georgie and the Dragon · **Julia Jarman**
Cowardy Cowardy Cutlass · Free With Every Pack ·
Mo and the Mummy Case · The Fizziness Business ·
Robin Kingsland
And Pigs Might Fly! · Albertine, Goose Queen · Jigger's Day Off ·
Martians at Mudpuddle Farm · Mossop's Last Chance ·
Michael Morpurgo
Hiccup Harry · Harry's Party · Harry with Spots On ·
Chris Powling
The Father Christmas Trap · **Margaret Stonborough**
Pesters of the West · **Lisa Taylor**
Jacko · Messages · Rhyming Russell · **Pat Thomson**
Monty, The Dog Who Wears Glasses · Monty Bites Back ·
Monty Must be Magic · Monty – Up To His Neck in Trouble ·
Colin West
Ging Gang Goolie – It's An Alien! ·
Stone the Crows, It's a Vacuum-cleaner · **Bob Wilson**

First published in Great Britain by
A & C Black (Publishers) Ltd 1992
First published in Young Lions 1993
10 9 8 7 6 5 4 3

Young Lions is an imprint of the Children's Division,
part of HarperCollins Publishers Ltd,
77–85 Fulham Palace Road, London W6 8JB

ISBN 0 00 674357 9

Printed and bound in Great Britain by
HarperCollins Manfacturing, Glasgow

THIS IS UGATHA

She is a cave-girl.

And exactly six hundred and twenty thousand years ago last Tuesday at about half past four, she was a rather unhappy cave-girl.

For her mother had just asked her to do some dusting.

Why me?

Now when I tell you that just a few moments earlier Ugatha's mother had said to her brother:

And that Ugbert had replied:

An economy size mammoth.

Ugbert.

You might wonder what Ugatha was making such a fuss about.

But you've probably never had to dust a cave.
As you probably know, mammoth hunting is exciting and dangerous and fun. Dusting a cave is boring.
All that happens when you dust a cave is . . .

. . . you get very dusty!

Uncle Ugstein, who was sitting in the corner of the cave, trying to teach a dodo the basic principles of evolutionary survival, said . . .

'Stone the crows! I can't see a thing!'

Then he made a more interesting observation:

What you really need for that job is a vacuum-cleaner.

NB: Uncle Ugstein was not an average Stone Age caveman. He was more in the way of ...

A PROPHET AND A GENIUS!

He was without doubt
the Leonardo da Vinci of his age.

Ugatha's mother, however, didn't
know this.
Which explains why she said . . .

Ugatha, however, was by nature an inquisitive girl – and hated dusting. Which explains why she enquired . . .

A NOTE FROM THE AUTHOR.

You may think it odd that an intelligent girl like Ugatha had never heard of a vacuum-cleaner. BUT you must remember that Stone Age people didn't have all sorts of things that you and I take for granted.
FOR INSTANCE. THEY DIDN'T HAVE →

scissors, padlocks,

clothes-pegs, roller-skates,

suit-cases,

buckets,

helicopters,

knitting-needles,

mops,

atomic power stations,

candles,

tooth-paste, safety-pins,

hair-driers,

typewriters,

blowlamps,

10-speed mountain bikes,

chainsaws,

the wheel,

cameras,

hammers, riding boots, keys,

portable televisions, paint-brushes, cups and saucers, penknives, teddy-bears, mouse-traps, lawn-mowers, violins, 100-watt total output stereo-centres with a 3-band equalizer, goldfish bowls, anchors, electricity . . .

ANOTHER NOTE FROM THE AUTHOR

It's just occurred to me that it might actually be a bit simpler if I told you what Stone Age people did have.

WHAT STONE AGE PEOPLE DID HAVE WAS..

STONES

The average Stone Age cave person thought that stones were the best thing since sliced mud.

But Uncle Ugstein was not an average cave person.

He knew somehow that somewhere there might be such materials as plastic and polythene and polywollydoodle-oodle-polyput-the kettle-on, and that these materials might someday be made into useful domestic appliances.

Even so, it's very odd that he should have mentioned a vacuum-cleaner at that precise moment, because . . .

. . . at that precise moment, six hundred and twenty thousand years in the future, at about ten minutes to five, in a place which had once been called . . .

"A PILE OF STONES, NEAR A RATHER DUSTY CAVE"

. . . but which, since the invention of reading, writing, sign-posts, and the Collins Motoring Atlas, had been called:

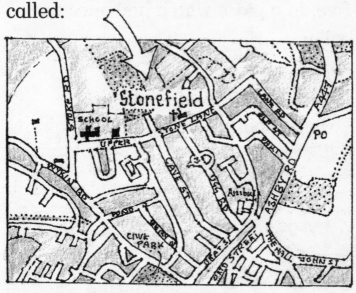

A young girl called Doreen Pegg was wondering what to do for her Summer science project.

DOREEN PEGG

was by nature an inquisitive girl.

Eleven plus thirteen equals twenty-four.

Please, Miss.

Yes, Doreen?

Why?

And she was not short of confidence.

I'm going to be the very first Nobel Peace Prize winning ballerina to write a best-selling book about how playing goalkeeper for Manchester United helped her to become the only governor of the Bank of England to have climbed Mount Everest wearing stiletto heels

So, it's not really surprising that she decided to have a go at question 2b.

Stonefield Park
PRIMARY SCHOOL

Cave Avenue
Stonefield
Pebbleston
Staffs
ST10 2HP

Headmaster   Mr J Wood

SUMMER SCIENCE PROJECTS.

Choose one from the following:-

1(a)   Grow a bean shoot in a
       jam-jar lined with soggy
       pink blotting paper.

 (b)   Make a musical instrument
       out of simple objects you
       find around the house.

2(a)   Make a weather chart
       showing daily temperatures
       and rainfall in the form
       of a graph.
       Draw any interesting clouds
       that you see, and make a
       note of what sort of weather
       they bring.

 (b)   Build a time machine.

TIME

. . . from the time it first began* Man
had been intrigued by it. What was
it? Where was it? And, if it waited for
no man, what was the point of it
anyway?

Unless you could measure it and call
it something simple, time was a bit
of a waste of er . . . time.

What is
The Time?

An abstract philosophical
concept which relates
to successive states of
the universe.

Ancient man built huge stone circles and used the shadow of the sun as a means to record the passing of the days.

Renaissance man devised more sophisticated ways to mark the passing of the hours.

Modern man, for what it's worth, can now measure time to less than a billionth of a second.

What's the exact time, professor?

One billionth of a second past... sorry, two billionths of a sec... No, sorry, three...

Modern man can make atomic clocks, watches that tell the time underwater, and timers which will switch the video on at half past two a week next Thursday.
AND YET . . . despite all these technological advances there's one thing that man still can't do with time, and that is travel backwards through it. The nearest he's got up to now is . . .

The railway timetable.

> The fast train for Crewe, due to depart at 23.58 will not now arrive until 01.05. Passengers are advised to catch the 01.42 slow train which will reach Crewe ten minutes earlier.

It occurred to Doreen that as far as time-travel was concerned, Man had been a bit of a failure. She said to herself . . .

It's about time a woman had a go.

Doreen decided that Man, as usual, had been trying to be too clever. Complicated problems often had simple solutions. What was needed to solve this problem was obvious.

All that was needed was – an alarm-clock, a vacuum-cleaner, and a bit of common sense.

She set the vacuum-cleaner controls to super-turbo-suck . . .
. . . and switched on.

There was a big flash...
(which looked a bit like this)

AND THEN . . .

...AT THE SPEED OF LIGHT. WH...
1583 BC... Oh, Mr Bell, Good of you to ring.
knox! knox!
Who's there?
What arrow? I can't see an arrow.
Bayeux!
HARO
Alp! It's Hannibal and his wooden elephant!
Friends, Romans and round heads. Lend me your ears.
What did he say?

UNTIL AT LAST . . .

29

She landed on a pile of stones, near a rather dusty cave.

Seeing a rather hairy caveman nearby she decided to ask him where and when she was.

> Excuse me.

Now, sometimes when people meet a stranger for the first time they're not quite sure what to say.

But when Uncle Ugstein met Doreen
for the first time, and particularly
when he saw that she had with her
the very same domestic cave-cleaning
appliance that only minutes earlier
he had predicted would one day exist,
he knew exactly what to say.

he exclaimed.

When Doreen pointed out that the thing she had on her head was not in fact, a vacuum-cleaner, but an alarm-clock, Uncle Ugstein was rather put out.

But when she explained what an alarm-clock was for, and what it did he smiled at Doreen, and said:

When she heard how Ugbert usually got people to wake up . . .

. . . Doreen was inclined to agree.

Uncle Ugstein was very pleased to meet Doreen; it was good to talk about the future with somebody who knew what she was talking about. He took her to the cave to meet Ugbert and the rest of the family. They made her feel very welcome.

Doreen got on particularly well with Ugatha; she and Doreen found that they too had much in common.

As the sun began to set behind the mountains, Doreen turned to Ugatha and said:

'What do you do of an evening?'

'We bump into things,' said Ugatha. Then she added:

'Sometimes, if it's cold, we huddle around Uncle Ugstein's camp fire.'

'You've got a camp fire?!' said Doreen, not a little surprised.

'Can I see it?'

'Of course,' said Uncle Ugstein.

Now, as a precaution, (in case she ended up in the dark ages), Doreen had brought with her a box of matches.

When she explained what matches were, and what they did, Uncle Ugstein beamed at her and said:

When she heard how Ugbert had been trying to light the fire . . .

. . . Doreen was inclined to agree.

She explained that setting fire to a pile of stones was rather difficult, even with a box of matches. Setting fire to sticks was easier.

And so it was that Man (and woman) first discovered fire.
A discovery which led to another of the most important discoveries in the civilization of mankind . . .

The dinner party.

Next thing you know we'll be discovering washing-up.

Doreen said that she thought that this was the perfect end to a very interesting day.
And Ugatha agreed.

But there was something that Ugatha hadn't told Doreen about.

She had forgotten to tell her about
the other thing that cave people
often did at night when it went dark.

The other thing that cave people
often did at night when it went dark
was . . .

...GET EATEN BY... A SABRE-TOOTHED TIGER!

You've probably never been eaten by a sabre-toothed tiger.

Have you ever wondered why?

THE SABRE-TOOTHED TIGER.

An expert answers your questions.

Q Are sabre-toothed tigers fierce?

A Yes

Q How fierce?

A In terms of pure animal fierceness most experts would classify the sabre-toothed tiger as being: really, very, ooooh!, ever-so, steaming Ada just look at the size of his teeth, fierce.

Q Do they eat people?

A Yes

Q How come I've probably never been eaten by one then?

A Because you don't see them around much nowadays.

Q Why not?

A Because they're extinct.

Q Why did sabre-toothed tigers become extinct?

A Most experts believe that sabre-toothed tigers became extinct because they could not adapt to changes in the natural environment.
As a consequence of this they were unable to obtain an adequate supply of the food which they required in order for them to sustain their normal life-style.

Q Could you illustrate that?

A Certainly.

This is the type of environment in which a sabre-toothed tiger could flourish.

Q You mean that the only reason sabre-toothed tigers died out was they didn't know how to cross the road in order to get to a Burger Bar?

A Well, not the only reason.

Q There was another reason?

A Yes.

Q Had this other reason got something to do with the fact that there was insufficient intra-specific variety arising from

naturally occurring mutations
within the genetic make up of
the species such as would allow
for a macro-mutative adaptation
to a suitable ecological niche
within the changed environment?

A **No. It had something to do with
Doreen Pegg's vacuum-cleaner.**

Q What on earth d'you mean!?

A **If you carry on reading the
story you'll find out.**

Supper being over, Doreen and her new friends were now having a quiet chat around the fire.

She couldn't help noticing that cave people were not very good at knowing what things were called.

She decided to put them right.

You mean to say this isn't a.. 'Chuckitatit'?

No. That's called a 'lump of rock'.

She's a walking dictionary.

What's that?

No idea.

Doreen was just about to explain that a very, very, very, big stone was called – 'A boulder', and that lots of little rounded stones were called – 'Pebbles', when from quite nearby there came a strange 'grrrrrrraghling' sound.

'What's that?' Doreen enquired.

'Well now,' said Ugatha.

'No, it's not,' said Ugbert.

'In actual fact,' said Uncle Ugstein.

Uncle Ugstein never finished his sentence.

YET ANOTHER
NOTE FROM THE AUTHOR

I think what Uncle Ugstein was going to say was this : —

Sometimes it doesn't matter if you don't know what a thing is called.

Sometimes it's more important to know what it does.

And sometimes, especially if the thing is just about to do what it does, it's really important to know what you should do before it goes and does it.

Uncle Ugstein never got around to finishing his explanation. After what happened next he didn't need to.

What happened next, and what they did about it was . . .

49

Now this was the very first time that Doreen had ever been cornered in a cave by a raging mad, ravenous, sabre-toothed tiger.

So, as you might expect, she was rather interested to know what cave people usually did in such circumstances.

'Well,' said Ugatha's mother. 'If my memory serves me correct, what my sister Ugwin and her family did the last time they were cornered in a cave by a mad, ravenous, sabre-toothed tiger was . . .

. . . get torn to shreds.

Ugbert said:

If I'd got a 'Bashitsheadin' I could bash its head in.

But I've only got this primitive club.

And Ugatha said:

If I'd got a 'Chuckitatit' I could chuck it at it.

But I've only got this lump of rock.

But Uncle Ugstein, being a prophet and a genius, and an inventor, and the Leonardo da Vinci of his age, said: 'I know what we need!'

53

Ugatha's mother said:
'Take no notice of Uncle Ugstein.
He's round the twist.'

But Doreen said:
'No he's not. He's given me an idea.'

What Uncle Ugstein had said had
made Doreen think of something. It
had made her think about . . . the
milkman, the postman, and the man
who came to read the electricity
meter – and the thing that they'd all
got in common.

They were all terrorised by next-door's alsatian.

It was a raging mad, ravenous beast.
The electricity man said it was mad.
The milkman said it was ferocious.
Once, it had torn the postman's trousers to shreds.
BUT . . . there was one thing that this ravenous, raging mad, ferocious, trouser-shredding beast was afraid of.
One thing it couldn't stand.
One thing it always ran away from.
It was the one thing that all animals seem to be afraid of.
Doreen said:

Listen everybody! I've had an idea. What we do is......

And what they did was . . .

And it worked!
And from that day forth, whenever
cave people were threatened by wild
beasts, they pretended to be doing
the vacuum-cleaning. And every
time, the wild beast would run off,
and race around in a mad panic,
trying to find a table to hide under.

And they never could find a table to
hide under because . . .
tables hadn't been invented yet!

And that's the other reason why
sabre-toothed tigers became extinct.

And you probably don't believe me.

THE DOREENIAN THEORY OF EVOLUTION

An expert answers your questions.

Q Do you really expect me to believe that lots of animals became extinct because they wore themselves out trying to find a table to hide under?

A Yes

Q What scientific evidence have you got to support this daft theory of yours, eh?

A Take a fresh look at these prehistoric cave paintings

Here we see a painting found in the Magoura cave in Bulgaria. It clearly shows a man with an imitation Hoover (upright model 355) putting the wind up an emu.

This painting, from Adjefou in the Sahara desert, shows two men with vacuum-cleaners scaring off a sabre-toothed tiger.*

The man at the back is probably Uncle Ugstein, though what he's doing with an imitation ironing-board is anybody's guess.

Now read on. ⇨

* Notice that there are no signs of a table anywhere.

Doreen helped the cave people with some of their other problems too. For example, she helped . . .

Uncle Ugstein with his inventing.

Ugatha's mother with her washing.

And she would have helped Ugatha with the problem she was having with stopping the alarm-clock . . .

... but Ugbert arrived with his bashitsheadin and before she could stop him ...

and suddenly ...

SHE FOUND HERSELF BACK [...]

Doreen. There you are.
I've been calling you for ages.
Why didn't you answer?
You promised to help me with the dusting.
Where on earth have you been?

What should she say?

She wanted to say:
I've been exactly six hundred and twenty thousand years away. I've been living with a family of Stone Age cave people.
I've been teaching them how to make fire, and invent the wheel.
We had a dinner party, and then afterwards we fought off a raging mad, ravenous sabre-toothed tiger with a vacuum-cleaner.
As it happens, Mum, I've probably been changing the whole course of history and evolution.

But she had an idea that her mother wouldn't quite believe her.

So she said the only thing she knew her mother <u>would</u> believe.

Isn't it funny the odd things some people will choose to believe.